Edge of Eternity

By Shiree Walker

DEDICATION

All gifts come from above. I dedicate this, my first book, to my Lord and Savior, Jesus Christ. Without Him, I would be nothing.

Contents

Acknowledgements

I would like to thank my wonderful husband, Brian for his help and support through this process, and for being my editor. Thanks to my beautiful children, Bethany, Erin, and Caleb for their patience and for not tearing the house down as I pursue my dream of writing. I would also like to thank Tara Schurz Shields for designing my lovely cover! Many thanks also to Pat and Enlow Walker for their love and support and for being the best parents-in-law ever!

Chapter 1: A Day in the Life of Emily

Gradually...through the pounding in my groggy head, I'm aware that someone is calling my name... knocking on my bedroom door. I squint my eyes, straining to focus on anything in the dim light. Then, standing in front of my bed, are my mother's slippers. They look more fuzzy than usual this morning. Everything does. I don't raise my eyes to look at her face. I don't want to see the look of disappointment I know will be there.

"Emily, it's noon. I think you should get up." She says sternly.

"Mom... just give me a few minutes, will you?" I grumble, rolling over to face the wall and squeezing my eyes shut.

"Emily, you did this to yourself. Now come on." She yanks my blanket off and throws it on the floor.

I shiver and groan. My head throbs as I sit up, cradling it in my hands.

"Was it really worth it?" she asks incredulously.

"Ugh..." is all I can get out.

Edge of Eternity

Why can't she just let me be? I'm an adult now - I can make my own decisions. I can't wait until college starts, then I can do what I want without being pestered about it!

"Take a shower. I'll make some coffee." She says as she opens the blinds, pouring in the painful light of mid-day!

"Mom!" I yell, covering my eyes as I stagger over and shut the blinds again.

She leaves me to suffer in peace, for now...

I trudge down the hallway to the bathroom, hoping it isn't occupied by either of my younger siblings. To my relief the entire upstairs of our house seems to be abandoned, so I can go about my "morning" routine uninterrupted.

I glance at the mirror in the bathroom and startle myself! Wow! I'm a mess! I was too exhausted when I got home last night, er...this morning, that I just went to bed without bothering to remove my makeup. My mascara is smudged, enhancing the bags that hang beneath my eyes, and my bright lipstick has rubbed off in places. I look like death warmed over... I really hope I can pull myself together before my date tonight!

I open the medicine cabinet and snatch the bottle of Ibuprofen off the shelf. I try to get my eyes to focus enough to line up the little child-proof arrows on the cap and finally pop it off. I dump four tablets into my hand and pop them into my mouth, cupping some tap water in my hands to wash them down. I really hope they kick in soon! I place the bottle back on the shelf and spy the acetaminophen - better take a couple of those, too.

Having medicated myself, I hop into the shower, letting the hot water wash away all the grime from last night's party. Summer vacation... the last one before I start college and begin life on my own... I intend to enjoy every second of it!

For a long time I stand there, just letting the hot water run over me. I don't feel like being rushed. Eventually the water begins to feel tepid, and I finish rinsing my hair in a hurry. When I finally get out of the shower, a full hour has passed and it is after 1pm. I wrap up in my cuddly bath robe and head downstairs, hoping maybe Mom will take pity on me and feed me some breakfast.

Downstairs, everything is quiet. Mom must have gone out. Probably too angry to talk to me right now. I don't understand why things bug her so much. She got to live her life the way she wanted, right? Why can't I?

I rummage around in the fridge for something to eat, pulling out some leftover spaghetti and meatballs they must have had for dinner last night. Spaghetti for breakfast... why not? Anyways, technically it's lunch time, so, perfectly acceptable!

I pour myself some coffee while my meal is warming in the microwave and breathe in the rich aroma... Coffee... One of mankind's greatest discoveries! The microwave beeps and I remove my bowl of spaghetti, almost dropping it on the floor as my delayed senses realize that the bowl is blistering hot! Ouch! Maybe I shouldn't have left it in for quite that long...

I sit down at the dining room table, gazing out the large, bay windows at the manicured lawns and fancy houses of our cushy neighborhood. Yes, this is the life... Someday, when I get through medical school, I'm going to have my own place, just like this.... Maybe even better!

I smile at the thought as I sip my coffee... Yes, soon I'll have to start taking life more seriously... but not today.

On the island in the kitchen, I spy my brother, Reuben's laptop. Mine is upstairs in my room. I don't want to go get it... What he doesn't know won't hurt him. I get up with a groan and let the world stop spinning before taking the long, five steps over to retrieve it. I then plop back down in my chair and caress my cup of coffee, taking a couple more sips before opening the laptop and hacking the password protection. My brother is so predictable...he always picks the easiest passwords to figure out. This time it's the name of his goldfish... Doesn't he know that's one of the first things I'd try? I grin evilly as his desktop loads and the picture of him with his little girlfriend pops up.

What was her name again? Oh yeah...Cynthia. Strange name. Strange girl. I think he could do better. But he doesn't ask me, and doesn't appreciate my advice. I've got two whole, extra years of dating experience - he could learn a lot from me if he'd listen.

Sure...I've made some mistakes when it comes to love...who hasn't? I'm doing things right this time with Chase. I've had my heart broken too many times...well, twice... and it isn't going to happen again. I like Chase a lot. We have fun together, but we both know we're going to college. Relationships just don't hold up over time and distance...that's just the way it is. The less emotionally involved we become, the easier it will be to say goodbye. I don't know that Chase 'gets it' like I do.

To be honest...I think he's falling in love with me. The thought makes me sad. I don't want to hurt him - I told him at the beginning of our relationship that we couldn't be serious. I hope he understands and won't be bitter if I break things off at the end of summer break.

I pull up Facebook and start scrolling through my brother's newsfeed. Why does he have such dumb friends? And then there's the church crowd he keeps on here, posting community events and charitable causes. My brother has always been such a "good" boy. In church, on time, in his best church clothes, every Sunday. Going to all the youth camps and events, attending Bible studies. There's still hope he'll grow out of it, like me...

Finally bored with my brother's Facebook account, I post something "shocking" on his wall and sign out. Let's see how long it takes him to find out he was hacked! I chuckle to myself...Classic...just classic...

I'm working on my second cup of coffee when I hear the front door open. I crane my neck around to see who just came in, squinting to make out the figure in the dimness of the hallway.

"Dad! You're home!" I say with my sweetest smile.

"Hey, Emily. How's my girl?" He greets me as he strolls over, squeezing me around the shoulders and planting a kiss on my forehead.

"I'm good, Dad." I say, trying to appear cheerful, and like my head isn't about to explode.

"Had a rough night?" He asks, a shadow creeping across his countenance.

"Do I look that bad?" I ask, covering my face with my hands and rubbing my eyes.

"You do look kind of bad…" He says, pouring himself the last cup of coffee.

"I love you, too, Dad!" I say with a huff, but I don't really mind him teasing me.

Dad and I have always been close. Some of my best childhood memories are the times we spent together, playing softball, fishing on the lake, picking out the constellations in the night sky… Those were good days, life was so simple. I miss that.

Dad sits down across from me at the table and picks up the newspaper, sipping his coffee as he glances over the headlines.

"It's a sad world, Emily…" He says, shaking his head.

"Yep." I reply, hoping the topic will expire.

"Sad, sad things happening all over the place… I'm so thankful that no matter what happens, we can count on our God to…"

"I have to go get dressed, Dad!" I interrupt him, standing up as quickly as I dare and heading to the sink to rinse off my dishes.

"Ok…" I hear him mutter, the disappointment in his voice almost making me sorry for not letting him finish the speech I've heard a hundred times.

I place my dishes in the dishwasher and head upstairs to my room. My headache is finally starting to ease with the aid of the medication and I can go about getting ready for the rest of the day.

I think Chase has something special planned for our date tonight, my heart beats a little faster anticipating what it might be! He's such a good, devoted, boyfriend… it's a shame he isn't going to the same college I am… who knows what might have happened? I like him a lot. I really do. He's handsome, kind-hearted, thoughtful, and puts me first, always… But, sometimes I feel like we're not on the same page in so many ways. I want to talk about a future career, and he keeps bringing up this "family" thing. I always shut that topic down quickly, but I can tell it means a lot to him. I think he will make a good family man someday, just not with me...at least not now. After medical school, who knows? Maybe our paths will cross again when the time's right.

Those things aside, tonight we're going to have fun! I smile at the thought as I begin blow drying and styling my naturally curly, brown, hair. I don't do much with my hair, just a basic dry and a little styling gel for body.

"Looking good, Emily..." I think to myself as I put on my earrings and begin applying my makeup. "No one would ever know you had a terrific hangover this morning! That Chase is a lucky man..." I smile with approval as I survey myself one last time, making a tiny adjustment to my eye-liner... Perfect!

My phone beeps somewhere in the room. I rummage around in the dirty clothes on the floor, searching for the pair of jeans I wore last night, my favorite ones with the sparkly rhinestones on the back pockets. A birthday gift from my parents... Ah! There they are! I dig my phone out of the back pocket and drop the jeans back onto the floor. Hmmm... I don't recognize the number... But it's in my contacts. Must be someone I met at the party last night. What do they have to say?

I tap the message icon and it opens up on the screen, "Epic party last night, huh? Txt me back if u wanna hang out again!"

There's an attachment that pops up with a selfie of a guy...he's kind of cute! I rack my brain trying to remember him! Some fuzzy memories float back in... I think I vaguely remember... Yeah, he was a funny guy! Maybe we could hang out a time or two...

But... No, I can't do that to Chase. I couldn't betray his trust. I want things to be good between us, even when it's over. He's my best friend...I don't want to hurt him, even though it's probably bound to happen.

Feeling good about myself, I head downstairs passing my little sister Kay, on the way down.

"Hey kiddo!" I ruffle her hair as I go past, she glares at me and tries to smooth it back down.

"Where were YOU last night?" She asks with a sneer.

"Wouldn't YOU like to know?" I sneer back teasingly.

She rolls her eyes, gives a huff, and is off to her room. Since when did she get so temperamental? A kid turns thirteen, and they're just no fun anymore! Oh well...

"See you later, Kay!" I holler at her from the bottom of the stairs.

"Katherine!" she shouts back at me.

Wow...something really ticked her off today! Must be those lovely teenage hormones... She'll probably be as sweet as pie tomorrow. Maybe I can take her to the mall later this week - she'd like that. She isn't allowed to go alone yet.

I grab my purse off the coat rack and turn the door handle, "Emily, wait!" my mom's voice calls out.

Oh no...here it comes... I sigh and let go of the handle. Dragging my feet down the hall and into the kitchen.

I brace myself for the lecture as Mom walks over to me, arms crossed. She looks down at the floor, and then straight into my eyes, making me uncomfortable. Then, she wraps me in a tight hug, catching me off guard!

"Emily, I love you. Don't forget that, ok?" She says, still hugging me tight.

"I know, Mom," I say, patting her on the shoulder, "I love you, too."

She lets go of me, and turns her attention back to the meal she's preparing. I glance over at the pot on the stove, minestrone... MMMmmm! One of my favorites! Too bad I won't be here for dinner.

"See you later, Mom!" I call as I head out the front door.

I breathe in the hot, summer air, heavy with the scent of the roses that adorn the flower bed in front of our house. The sun is dazzlingly bright and hurts my eyes. I dig around in my purse and pull out my sunglasses. Much better! I hit the unlock button on the key ring and hop into my car.

I drive over to my friend Brianna's house to pick her up. We've been planning a shopping trip for a few days now. I want a new outfit for my date tonight, and a couple of new outfits to take with me to college. I have some spending money from babysitting my cousins a few times recently. Aunt Linda always pays me a little extra - she's awesome!

I walk up to the door of Brianna's house and knock... There are voices inside - they sound upset! A bedraggled Brianna opens the door, a pout on her face.

"You're not ready? It's 3:30!" I scold her, teasingly.

"I can't go... I'm grounded." She says, rolling her eyes.

"Grounded? Seriously? You're seventeen years old!" I exclaim, shocked that her parents still bother with discipline at her age.

"Yep..." is all she says.

"How long are you grounded?"

"They said forever...but I think it's actually until my birthday, a month from now." She replies.

"That..." some choice, expressive words gather in my throat, but Brianna's mother's face appears behind her shoulder and I force them back down.

"I'll talk to you later." I say, heading back to my car.

"No, you won't!" Brianna's mother calls from the door, and my heart drops.

Is she really that upset? She can't possibly keep Brianna from talking to me for a whole month, can she? She must think I'm a bad influence, which is utterly ridiculous!

I shoot her a glare as I open my car door and slide in behind the wheel. She stares back at me with icy fortitude.

This is so overdramatic! It was just a little party! All young people party now and then! She really needs to lighten up... I never did like that woman!

I drive to the strip mall where the best clothes stores are, feeling angrier than I've felt in a really long time! Brianna is only a month away from being an adult. Don't they see that they can't control her life anymore?

"Humph!" I say as I pull into a parking space a lot farther away from the stores than I'd like.

I grumble and gripe about Brianna's mother all the way to the entrance of the store, calling her several distasteful names. The doors slide open, and temporarily, all my troubles melt away as I'm caught up in the excitement of shopping! This store has the coolest atmosphere, the best music, the most fabulous selection of cute outfits and accessories!

I make a couple of purchases, including a short, purple dress for my date tonight. This is going to look great with my red high heels and hoop earrings! I glance at the clock display on my cell phone - 4:45! I need to get home and change! I'll be late for my date!

It's ok...Chase won't mind waiting a few extra minutes. It will be totally worth it!

On the drive home, the drama with Brianna and her mother doesn't even cross my mind. I'm thinking about Chase... Playing through the scenario at summer's end. I'm truly fond of him, but I know I don't love him. If I loved him, I'd try to figure out a way for a long distance relationship to work. But I don't want to be tied down to someone while I'm in college. I want the freedom to explore and meet new people. Maybe I'll find someone I TRULY love, and things will be different. But it isn't Chase, I know that. And...he needs to know, too.

The longer I keep this relationship going, the harder the break-up will be. I need to get it over with. But it's easier said than done...breaking someone's heart. The thought sobers me some, and I do my best to push it away. There's no need to ruin our date tonight, I still have several weeks to figure this all out.

Edge of Eternity

I swing into our driveway and skip up to the house, my recent purchases hanging in their pretty, colorful, paper bags on my wrist.

As I open the door, I'm greeted by my brother's angry voice, "Emily! Don't touch my Facebook account! That's not even funny!"

"Sure it is." I reply with a grin, heading up the stairs.

As I go, I can hear him mumbling as he's typing, "I was hacked, I was hacked, hacked, hacked!"

I snicker to myself...it just never gets old.

Chapter 2: Save the Date

It's 5:45 and Chase is downstairs talking to my brother, which is good. They seem to get along really well. I put the final re-touches on my makeup and survey the finished product in the mirror… Perfect! I can't wait to see his face! I slip on my high heels and open the door to my bedroom. Kay is standing there, this time she's smiling.

"You look pretty, Emily!" She says sweetly.

"Thank you… What do you want?" I ask suspiciously.

"Ummm… I was wondering if you had twenty dollars I could borrow? Mom said 'No' and I really need it for something!" She pleads with her big, blue eyes staring up at me…

I feel myself caving in.

"May I ask what it's for?" I say, raising an eyebrow.

"It's really none of your business!" She snaps, and then catches herself.

"Pleeeaaase, Emily! I really NEED it, just this one time! I'll pay you back when I get my allowance! I promise!" She whines, clasping her hands together.

She looks so pitiful... I dig into my purse and hand her the cash.

"I want it back on Saturday." I say sternly.

"Yes, Emily! Thank you!" She skips off, and I smile.

"You're welcome." I say to her back as she disappears into her room.

I daintily prance down the stairs in my heels. Chase raises his eyes to mine, and the look on his face nearly melts my heart. His warm smile and shining eyes light up his face, all for me... It's obvious he adores me. I feel a twinge of guilt, wishing I could feel the same way for him...

"Emily, you look stunning!" He raves as I take his outstretched hand.

"Thank you." I say smiling, diverting my eyes from his intense gaze.

"Go on, you two!" My brother grumbles, "Keep the mush to yourselves!"

I stick my tongue out at him as we head out the door, arm in arm.

Chase opens the passenger door of his Toyota Tacoma for me and I climb in as gracefully as I can. He hops in on the driver's side and starts the engine. I stare at him a moment as he puts the truck in reverse and tries to talk about the weather. He's acting jittery, like on our first date... A sinking feeling starts to creep over me... Something's up.

I wait expectantly for him to pull into the parking lot of one of the nicer restaurants in town, but he drives right past them and heads toward the highway.

"Where are we going?" I ask curiously.

"It's a surprise..." He says with a smile, "You'll like it."

"Ok..." I say as we pass the last few businesses and head out of town.

Edge of Eternity

We drive another half-hour or so and I begin feeling a little anxious. My parents don't expect me to be going anywhere far from home... What if Chase has been a psycho in disguise all this time?!

I study his face as he looks over at me adoringly... No, I don't think he's a psycho... But I thought he knew I was a city girl. What does he think I'll enjoy out here? We exit the main highway and drive up a bumpy logging road. I feel like grumbling, but don't want to spoil Chase's surprise, so I bite my lip.

Finally, we stop at the end of the little road, if you could call it a road, and Chase helps me out of the truck.

"What are we doing here?" I ask, trying to sound optimistic.

"You'll see." he says mysteriously.

I watch as he pulls a picnic basket out from behind the driver's seat. I breathe a sigh of relief... A picnic... that doesn't sound too bad.

He holds the basket in one hand, and takes my hand with the other, leading me up a steep trail that climbs to the top of the mountain... Great. I wish he'd have warned me about this! I'd have chosen different shoes! Men... why can't they think of things like that?

He seems to sense my struggle, perhaps due to the occasional whine or groan I can't contain anymore.

"I'm sorry, Emily..." he says, blushing, "I didn't think to tell you to wear hiking boots."

"That's ok..." I pant, "I'm doing fine. Just fine..."

Without another word, he hands me the basket, scoops me up in his strong arms, and begins carrying me up the steep trail.

I smile with my arms wrapped tightly around his neck - this IS rather romantic! I lean my head on his shoulder and breathe in the smell of his after-shave, his clean T-shirt, and a hint of perspiration... I guess I'll overlook that since it's probably due to him carrying me!

He struggles up the path, and I feel a little bad for him. But I don't offer to walk - this was his idea, anyway.

13

He finally comes to a branch in the path that veers off and leads us out of the trees and along a steep drop-off. Wow… what a view! There is a fantastic gorge below us, with a clear, mountain stream which tumbles over boulders and fallen trees. As we continue on our way, I can hear the distant, crashing roar of a waterfall.

The path is a little close to the edge for my comfort and I ask him to put me down, fearing the extra weight will make him lose his balance and teeter off! He looks relieved as he sets me on my feet and takes my hand again.

"It's not much farther!" He wheezes.

"Good…" I grumble under my breath.

The path winds through some tall fir trees and then ends in a level rocky clearing overlooking the fantastic waterfall!

To my delight, I spy a table and two chairs, already set up in a mossy area with a clear view of the falls and rocky gorge below. There's a pretty tablecloth and unlit candle on the table, and I turn and smile at Chase, who is watching expectantly for my reaction.

"Do you like it?" He asks anxiously.

"Of course! It's great!" I reply, doing my best to sound delighted.

I can tell he put a lot of work and planning into this date, even though it's not really my sort of thing.

I walk over and take my seat at the table, which is sprinkled with tree dust and a couple of bird droppings…

It's so much cooler here than in the city, and the mist from the waterfall makes me feel a little chilly in my short dress.

Chase looks at the soiled tablecloth with dismay, snatches it off, gives it a shake, and turns it over so the clean side is up. He places the candle back in the center of the table and lights it with a trembling hand. I smile as he opens the basket and sets out two plates, two cans of soda, napkins, silverware, and a meal I wouldn't have expected him to be able to put together! There are perfectly breaded chicken strips, grapes, cheese, crackers, and a somewhat mushed, but tasty looking chocolate pudding pie.

"This looks delicious, Chase! I didn't know you cooked!"

"There are still a few things you don't know about me!" He says with a grin as he takes his seat across from me.

I chuckle as I daintily place my napkin on my lap and look greedily at the food on my plate. Without further ado, I scarf down the food on my plate, barely saying a word. I am starving after our trek up the mountain! As I finish the last bite of pie, I glance over at Chase's plate and realize he's barely touched his food!

"Is something wrong?" I ask surprised, as he usually has a hearty appetite.

"No… nothing." He says, staring down at his plate awkwardly.

The sinking feeling creeps back over me… this is it, something's wrong. I stare at him with wide eyes, waiting for him to tell me what's on his mind.

"Emily… I've been wanting to ask you this for a long time now…" He begins, and I feel my chest start to tighten up. "Emily, I know you have some reservations about marriage, and that your education is very important to you. It's important to me, too. Your happiness is all that matters to me…" He pauses and looks into my eyes.

I hope he can't detect the terror that I feel right now as I realize where he's going with all this!

"I want to support you, no matter what you dream of doing. I want to be a part of your life, and for you to be a part of mine, always…" He pauses to slide out of his chair, and gets down on one knee on the mossy rocks in front of me.

"Emily, what I'm asking is…"

I feel my lower lip starting to tremble and I struggle to keep myself from screaming for him to stop! Please, Chase, don't ask me!

"Emily Jean Watson, will you marry me? Will you let me be a part of your dreams?" he asks with a shaky voice and face blushed beet red.

"Chase..." I begin, diverting my eyes to a patch of moss on the ground, "I...I..." I stammer, trying to think of the right words, but they won't come!

I look back at his face, he looks as though he might explode with anticipation! What do I say? What?!

"Chase, I can't!" I blurt out.

I watch as his countenance falls, and he lowers his gaze to the ground.

"I'm not ready to get married, yet. I need time to experience life, and to figure out who I am. I'm sorry..." I say, getting up.

I watch as pain fills his eyes and I can tell he's holding back tears. I can't bear to watch him hurt like this! I spin around towards the path down the mountain and flee the agonizing scene. Tears fill my eyes and cloud my vision. I stumble once, regain my footing, and keep running!

I didn't want it to work out like this! This is just horrible!

"Emily!" I hear Chase call after me.

I keep running, nearing the steep part of the path by the edge of the gorge. I'm too upset to worry about the danger, I can't make myself slow down! I can barely see the path now, tears are streaming down my cheeks and stinging my eyes as they mix with my thick mascara. Then my right heel catches on a stone jutting out of the ground and I feel myself falling, terror seizes me as I realize I can't catch myself this time! I see the ground open up underneath me, and hear the rushing water as it grows closer.

It all happens too fast for me to think anything but "This is going to hurt..."

And it does...I feel myself collide with something hard and continue to tumble, hitting another object, then another! Pain upon pain hits me so fast that I can't distinguish one blow from the next! I can vaguely hear Chase screaming my name from the edge of the cliff above. Then I feel the icy water envelope my lower body, and my head strikes something hard where I stop… everything goes black, and the pain fades away…

Chapter 3: Path to Life

I flicker in and out of consciousness, barely aware of what's going on around me. I know I should probably be in a lot of pain, but I feel nothing. I must be hurt really bad…

I feel Chase lift me out of the water and cradle me in his arms, sobbing… He dials a number on his phone, and…I'm gone again.

Then there are voices, other voices all around me. But I can't open my eyes to see who they are. I must be out for a long time, because the next thing I'm aware of is the smell of a hospital, and the steady   beeping sound of my heartbeat on a monitor. My head throbs and the pain is so severe, I lose consciousness again.

This time, when I wake up, I am not in the hospital…I open my eyes and find myself standing alone, in a field of wildflowers. It appears to be dawn, and I shiver as a chilling breeze whips around my body.

"Where am I?" I say aloud, feeling confused…

Then, a voice from behind startles me, "Child of man," I spin around to see a shining form, a being unlike anything I've ever imagined!

He - at least I suppose it is a he - is standing there, staring at me with eyes the color of ice, in a face the hue of gold. His expression is not sympathetic, or hostile - it is a strange, knowing expression, like he understands me more than I understand myself...

"Who are you?" I ask him shakily.

My heart pounds in my chest and I feel weak in the knees, like I might crumple to the ground.

"Child of man, I have been watching you since the moment your life began. I have reported to He who created you all that has happened in your life since you took your very first breath. I was your guardian, until you reached the age of accountability. Since that time, I have been able to do nothing but watch as you stumbled, and fell away."

His words stab me like a knife... "Fell away..." Fell away from what? Then I realize... he means I've fallen away from God! Which means that if I'm dead, it must be too late! I didn't realize my path had taken me so far from God, but as I recall the choices I've made the last few years, I feel the grip of guilt around my throat like the cold fingers of death itself.

"Am I dead?" I squeak out, barely able to hear the words myself.

He looks at me earnestly, and I think I see his eyes soften, "No, child of man, not yet... But your time on the earth is drawing to a close."

"Then, where am I? Am I dreaming?" I ask, slapping myself in the face, hoping I'll wake up!

"You are within your own mind... caught between life and death. Here, you will be tested, and given one final chance to change the state of your heart and soul."

He points to the sun, just rising over the distant, purple mountains on the horizon. "When the sun sets," he then points to the west, which is still covered in long shadows so that I can't make out much of the terrain, "Your earthly body will cease to function, and you will enter into either eternal life... or eternal punishment..." His eyes are grave, and seem to grow darker as he speaks.

"That isn't enough time! I don't know what I'm supposed to do!" I cry, falling to my knees!

"All your life the answers you needed were right in front of you. They are already contained in your memories, written on your heart when you were a child. Find them again, Child of man, before it's too late... Stay on the path, it will lead you to what you seek." With that, he vanishes, leaving me alone.

The sun illuminates a land unlike anything I've ever seen. What a strange place this is! The sky is a pale violet color, the distant mountains in front of me are now a deep reddish hue in the growing light. The flowery meadow I'm standing in appears to have withered and died as soon as the light of the sun touched it. And then, a path appears. The light hits it and gives it a golden appearance. It continues in a straight line, as far as the eye can see.

I see now in the growing light that the meadow I stand in does not continue far. The path then cuts through some rolling hills and wooded areas, and farther in the distance loom ominous mountains which glow like they're on fire as the sun hits their peaks. I don't dare to imagine what might be hiding in those dark forests, or lurking on the rocks of the mountains. This is the path I must take, the only path to life!

I start out on the path, still feeling numb from all that has happened. Can I really be dying? I'm not ready to die! I have so many things I want to do! And what about Chase? I hurt him, and now he's going to feel responsible for my death...

The air is still chilly, and I shiver, hugging myself tightly with my arms. I walk slowly down the path and try to let the reality of what's happened sink in. I keep hoping I'll wake up back in my own bedroom and all of this will have just been a bad dream.

After walking a short distance, I come to a marsh where giant flowers spring from the boggy ground. They have the most beautiful, alluring scent, more lovely than any perfume I've ever smelled. Their petals are deep violet or crimson, with heart shaped spots adorning the centers. I stop on the path to admire them. I feel tempted to step closer to examine them, and breathe in their tantalizing aroma...

But, as I study them more carefully, I notice that the flowers' centers bear an eerie resemblance to the shape of a skull! Then, the flowers begin to dance around, the skull-like centers seem to grin and wink at me! I recoil, stepping back into the center of the path. There's definitely something wrong with these flowers! They're part of this strange world, and I have no idea what to expect from them.

I spy a small, white rabbit. It hops gingerly over to one of the massive blossoms, standing on its hind feet to sniff the blossom with its little, whiskered nose. Suddenly, like a flash, the flower snaps it's skull-like jaws down onto its unsuspecting victim and with a sickening squeak, the rabbit is gone! All of the flowers seem to dance with joy, and then turn their attention back to me!

I stagger away from the scene, then notice a sign next to the path which I hadn't noticed before. It reads, "The blossoms of worldly wisdom will pleasantly draw you into the jaws of death."

Ok... moving on. Goosebumps cover my arms and legs - I'm not sure if they're from the cold, or from being really creeped out!

I walk maybe another quarter of a mile and come to a little, lean-to shack. There's an old man sitting on a blanket inside. He looks at me with grey eyes, sunken in with age, and his face sags with loose skin and wrinkles. A snaggle-toothed grin spreads across his face as he sees I've noticed him. I study him for a moment, his scraggly white hair and long beard cascade over his shoulders and chest. He's dressed in raggedy clothes and has bare feet that look like they haven't been washed in ages!

"Hi there, young lady!" he calls to me.

This could be another trick, I'd better ignore him.

"Could you be a dearie, and get me a cup of water from the spring across the way?" He points to a bubbling, little water fountain directly across the path from him.

I consider whether to help him or not. His shack is close enough to the path, I wouldn't have to step off of it to help him. But he's kind of creepy looking. I don't want to be bothered with this right now. My life is ticking away and I need to find my answers before it's too late.

"Sorry, I'm busy." I reply.

"Please. Help a poor, old man out. My joints don't allow me to do much moving around anymore. It will only take a moment." He pleads, holding out a tin cup for me to fill with water.

"Sorry." I say, shaking my head as I start walking again.

The smile disappears from his face, and so do all of his wrinkles! I stop and stare at him in astonishment as he transforms from the decrepit old man, into the dazzlingly bright form of the angel I first met on my arrival here.

"Child of man... You have failed to show kindness to a stranger in need. The path ahead of you will be difficult." He says with disappointment.

Then he vanishes, and I'm left to ponder his words. Oops... I guess I failed that test. This is hard! How do I know what I should, and shouldn't do? I can't take it back now, so I guess there's nothing to do but keep walking.

I haven't gone far before a strange scent is carried to my nostrils on the gentle breeze... it smells like smoke, and brimstone, and charred flesh! I turn my face against the breeze, to see where it's coming from.

To my horror, a monstrous creature, similar to a man but enormous, stands only a few yards away from me! Flames leap around his body as he stares at me with visible contempt! His glowing, yellow eyes seem to pierce through to my very soul. His muscular body from the neck down is covered in black scales, and he has golden, feathered wings like a bird of prey. I stumble and fall backwards in surprise, unable to regain my feet as I see him stride deliberately toward me.

He holds in one hand a massive heap of tangled chains and shackles, which make a loud jangling as he draws closer to me! I want to run, but I can't! I am frozen in place with fear - I can't even pull my gaze away from his burning eyes!

In his other hand, he holds a whip, with seven cords tipped with spikes. His feet have talons on them, like an eagle. His appearance is frightening, but not evil... In his countenance I see contempt, anger, and disappointment, but no pity, and no mercy!

Finally, I regain control of my limbs and begin scrambling down the path! I try to stand up and run, but I'm too shaky! I keep stumbling and flailing around on the ground. I hear his heavy footsteps right behind me! Unable to do much else, I curl up into a ball, covering my head with my arms and shutting my eyes tight!

The chains stop right beside me and he stands there, silently...

I feel the heat from his burning body and shudder, not sure whether to try and run again, or just remain where I am hoping he'll kill me quickly!

"Emily..." He says my name in a way which commands my attention.

I scream and try to crawl away, but he puts a massive foot down on my ankle, sinking his sharp talons into my flesh and scorching my skin! I cry out in pain, and there's nothing I can do but turn around to face him.

"What do you want? Who are you? " I shriek at him, trying futilely to free myself.

"I am Justice! My duty is to punish the wicked!" I look up at him, eyes wide with terror.

"But... I'm NOT wicked! I've never hurt anyone!" I whimper.

He looks at me in surprise. "Every sin against your Creator is worthy of death. That is justice. No unclean person can enter the Heavenly Realm. And you...reek of sin!" He says with disgust.

"These chains," he holds them up where I can see them clearly, "Are to shackle you forever to your sins. This whip," he holds up his other hand so I can see it clearly, "...is for your back, which you turned on your Creator and He who died for you. The burning fire shall be your home, and pain and misery your only companions."

"Please! Give me one more chance!" I cry out, still desperately trying to wrench my ankle from beneath the searing weight of his limb.

"When evening draws to a close, you will be mine to torment for all eternity!" He bends his face close to mine and the heat is nearly unbearable.

23

"Stumble off the path, and I will take you sooner!" He gives me a long, menacing stare, removes his foot from my ankle, and turns and strides away, dragging the mass of chains behind him.

I watch as he leaves the path, casting me one last threatening glance, and then disappears from sight behind a grove of trees. I clutch my burned foot and ankle, sobbing and rocking back and forth trying to work through the pain. I look up and see the sun has risen farther into the sky, it's bright rim peeking over the tops of the mountains in the east. I only have until evening - I can't let that creature take me! I force myself to get up and limp down the path, favoring my ankle that throbs with pain!

At least the going is not hard, the ground is fairly level and the path is straight. The grassy meadow is all burned and charred now, and the breeze which was cool before has become hot and dry, causing my burns to sting even more. After about a mile or so, I spy a small water fountain beside the path. I approach it and notice, engraved on a stone, the word "Courage".

I'm parched from the heat and take a long drink from the fountain. The water is cool and sweet, and I feel much better having re-hydrated myself. I also cup some water in my hands and trickle it onto my burns, which feel instant relief! I watch with wonder as if by magic, the burn on my ankle heals and fades away...

I am startled to see my Guardian, standing a short distance off.

He looks at me approvingly and says, "It takes courage to follow the path." Then he disappears, and I'm alone again.

I peer down the path and see that the meadow is coming to an end, and I must pass through a forest so thick that it's dark inside, even in the daylight.

"I could definitely use some courage about now..." I say to myself, taking one more sip of water before continuing on my way.

At the edge of the trees, I stop and stare down the dark path, trying to make out any threats that might be waiting for me. I can hear things, rustling around in the bushes and crashing through the trees on either side of the path. I swallow hard, take a deep breath, and cautiously enter the tree-line.

Edge of Eternity

I'm startled by a deep, thud behind me and spin around to see a black wall, reaching up to the sky blocking the path where the meadow was! I put my hands on the wall - it's cold and unyielding like stone. No turning back, now... I'm one step closer to the end of my journey...

I can no longer see the sun, and can't tell how much time passes as I trudge down the dark path, barely able to see it beneath my feet. Very little light filters through the branches of the massive trees which grow so close to the narrow path, I have to squeeze between them at times scraping my skin on their rough bark.

I try unsuccessfully not to scream as an occasional large insect or spider drops on me from the branches above! Strange noises emanate from both sides of the path - the snap of a twig, or rustling of something pushing through the undergrowth, and occasionally, a deep growl from some unseen beast. I dare not step foot off the path, or I'm sure I'll be devoured!

I have to get out of here! I quicken my pace as much as I dare, straining my eyes to see the path ahead of me.

Then, on the left side of the path, I see daylight streaming through a gap in the trees. The path branches into two - one path going hard to the left, the other continuing on, straight as an arrow... I am so tempted to rush out of this dreadful forest and evaluate things from there. Maybe I can skirt around the forest, and meet up with the straight path on the other side?

Then I recall the words of Justice, "Stumble off the path, and I will take you sooner!" I shudder at the thought.

No, I will stay on the straight path. Nothing I can face here will be as terrifying as being prisoner to that creature forever!

I look longingly at the light as I pass it, and proceed through the dark forest. The path ahead is pitch black now, I can see nothing. I do my best to walk in a straight line, hoping the path is still beneath my feet.

Then, a voice calls to me from somewhere in the trees... "Emily, come this way."

"Who are you?" I ask, not sure whether to be frightened, or encouraged...

"I'm a friend, I only want to help you on your journey. I can make your journey so much easier... trust me." The smooth, silky voice assures me.

"But, I'm not to leave the path." I reply, standing my ground.

"Come on, there's more than one way to reach your destination..." the voice replies, growing closer.

I strain my eyes into the blackness trying to make out the shape of who or what is speaking to me.

A strange, slithering sound makes its way towards me... and then there's a sharp hiss as it stops on the path next to me.

A gust of wind moves the tops of the trees above and a tiny glimmer of light breaks through the canopy... the light catches the many, smooth scales on the coiled body of a massive snake!

I may not know everything, but I know better than to trust a serpent!

I recoil from the creature in disgust and begin trudging down the dark path again, doing my best to ignore it's continued attempts to entice me. As I go, its hisses grow steadily angrier and it begins to spit and snap its jaws in frustration!

I go only a short distance, perhaps two hundred yards, before a light appears ahead of me! I made the right choice! I can see the way out of the forest now, and I run down the path, eager to be out in the open air again!

I rush out of the trees and into a clearing, nearly running right into a woman and her two children, sitting in the middle of the path.

"Whoa! Sorry about that!" I apologize.

"It's quite alright." The woman replies with a smile.

I glance back at the forest to see the gigantic serpent, standing like a cobra with its hood spread out. It writhes in anger as I turn away from it, breathing a sigh of relief.

"What are you doing here?" I ask, turning back to the woman on the path.

"My children and I are making our way home." She replies, looking down at the little, rosy cheeked cherubs huddled next to her.

"Are you following the straight path, too? Would you like to walk with me?" I ask, hoping to have some company.

"We'd love to!" She says warmly, getting up, and dusting herself off.

As she helps her two little ones do the same, I notice how old fashioned her clothes look - like from the "Leave it to Beaver" era... Hmmm... She isn't real either. None of this is... or is it? I don't know!

"I'm Emily..." I introduce myself, offering my hand.

"Charity," She shakes my hand gently, "and these are my children, Ignorant, and Ungrateful." She motions to the children, who both stare at me with wide eyes.

"Lovely names..." I say, trying not to snicker.

She smiles at the compliment, not catching the sarcasm behind it, and we head off down the path.

The going is nice and easy for a while and the children skip ahead, laughing, and pausing every now and then for us to catch up. I feel energized just watching them! We walk through a meadow with a little creek flowing through it, and here and there a sheep sleeps peacefully in the lush grass, or grazes near the water.

"What a pretty place!" I say to my companion.

"Yes, it is the Valley of Peace. It rests between the Forest of Confusion, and Mount Trial... We must enjoy it while we can." She says thoughtfully.

Far too soon, the meadow ends, and we stand at the base of an active volcano! Are you kidding me? Lava spews from the top and the ground beneath us shakes and rumbles! Fear grips my heart, and I don't know whether to go on, or to turn back!

I look behind me and to my shock, the meadow is on fire! The sheep have scattered, and standing on the path in the middle of the meadow, is the fiery figure of Justice! He's watching me! I can't turn back - I have to go forward, but how? I look at Charity, her eyes are fixed on the path in front of her. The children cling to her, crying and whimpering as she urges them on.

"Why did you bring us here?!" the older child, a girl about six years old, screams.

"This is stupid! You're stupid!" the girl stomps her foot and jerks away from her mother's grasp.

"Come on, Ungrateful..." the mother says gently, "You know home is on the other side of this mountain."

"Carry me, then!" Ungrateful says, crossing her arms and planting her feet firmly on the path.

I watch as Charity allows her child to climb onto her shoulders, and we attempt to continue up the path again.

"No! This isn't the way!" the other child, Ignorance, shouts.

"We must go this way, it's the only way." Answers Charity, tilting her head towards the path.

"Here, take my hand!" I offer, extending it the boy, who appears to be about four years old.

"No!" he shouts, pursing his lip and crossing his arms in front of him.

I glance back at the meadow. Justice is closer now, and the rattling of the chains dragging behind him grows louder as he makes his way towards us!

"Please! I'll help you! Come on!" I shout, beckoning to him, but the child doesn't budge.

Panicked, I snatch him up in my arms, hastening up the side of the mountain despite his angry screams and protests! He kicks, and beats on me as I carry him over my shoulder, struggling to keep my balance. Charity trudges on ahead of me, and I pant for breath and

28

stumble under my load. The path would be difficult to climb, even without having to carry these children!

Progress is slow, but we keep steadily on. I look back once or twice to see the tall, ominous figure standing at the base of the mountain, but he doesn't come up after us.

The mountain rumbles from deep within and the ground shakes so badly we are both knocked off balance and fall on our hands and knees. We scramble and claw to keep from tumbling back down the side of the mountain! After what seems like hours of struggling and climbing, we reach the summit of the mountain. We're standing only a stone's throw from a lava geyser that bubbles and hisses and threatens to shower us with molten rock at any moment!

"It's so hot up here! And I'm tired and hungry!" Ungrateful whines from her mother's back.

"We're almost home." Charity answers patiently, wheezing and struggling under the extra weight.

She falls to her knees more than once, bloodying them on the sharp stones, but continues on without complaint.

As we begin the steep descent down the other side of the mountain, I swing the boy, who's been pulling my hair and pinching my neck, off my shoulder and onto the path. To my shock, he takes off running, not down the path but toward the boiling lava!

"Stop!" I scream and bound after him, catching hold of his arm just as he stumbles and would have fallen to his death!

"What's wrong with you?" I scream at him, my heart pounding in my chest.

He looks at me dumbly and starts crying as I sling him over my other shoulder and make my wobbly way back to the path.

I shake my head as I stumble up beside Charity, who is waiting wide-eyed on the path.

"I'm so sorry." I say, feeling stupid.

"No harm done. Thank you for catching him." She says, giving me a weak smile.

We don't speak on the way down, aside from the occasional whimper or whine from the children. How can they be like this? Their mother and I are doing all the hard work, and yet they complain! What spoiled children! If I ever have kids... I begin to think, and then realize... I won't.

Tears well up in my eyes and I blink them back struggling to see the steep, rocky path in front of me. This is no time to cry. Remember what happened last time! As I recall the hurt in Chase's eyes, I feel the lump in my throat threaten to choke me! Again... I remind myself, this is not a good time to cry!

I swallow hard, and force myself to focus. Not too much farther!

Finally we reach level ground at the bottom and I swing the boy off my shoulder again, this time holding on tightly to his hand. Charity also lets the girl slide off her shoulders and scoops the little boy into her arms, hugging him tightly. The boy laughs and wriggles away, then the children are off! They skip down the path towards a small cottage not far from where we stand.

"They didn't even say thank you!" I hear myself grumble aloud.

I glance over at their mother, hoping she didn't notice!

She looks at me and shrugs, "I take care of them because I love them. I don't expect anything in return."

"But, doesn't it upset you that they behave like that?" I ask her, surprised.

"Of course, it hurts. But my love for them is unconditional. Just as my Savior's love for me is unconditional. He loved us, and died for us while we were sinners. He didn't die for us because we loved Him, but because He loved us. I hope and believe that someday my children will remember my love for them, and my example, and turn from their childish ways."

"Hmmm..." I process what she said, not knowing how to answer.

30

I never really thought about Jesus that way. I always assumed that He died for the good people, the church-goers who believe in Him. I hadn't considered that it was also for the bad people... Those who didn't even love Him. I guess I never really thought about it at all.

As we come to the little walk that leads to the cottage, Charity pauses and turns to me, "Safe Journey. May your road lead you safely home."

"Thank you." is all I can think to say.

She smiles, and turns towards the cottage where her children are waiting eagerly on the doorstep.

I stare after her until she reaches the door and turns to give me one last wave before disappearing inside.

Chapter 4: Hall of Mirrors

A farming district now stretches out before me, and beyond that, some more mountains. As I travel along the path, I realize that I'm starving! I didn't know you could be hungry in a dream...if this is a dream. I wonder if I'm hungry in real life right now? If so, eating something in this dream world won't really make a difference... Will it? I don't know, it doesn't matter! I just need to eat!

My pace has slowed considerably as hunger and fatigue catch up with me. My feet feel like weights as I pant and sweat, forcing myself to drag them forward, step by step... The sun beats down on me, making me feel wilted, and parched. How I'd love to lie down and rest for a bit... Even the fields of young wheat that ripple in the breeze look inviting, and I resist the temptation to collapse in their soft embrace... No, I can't sleep away the last few hours of my life! I yawn and continue on, struggling to keep my focus on the path ahead.

To the left of the path, I spy a roadhouse situated next to a sheer drop off. I stop when I reach it and take a moment to peer over the edge of the cliff... I can't see the bottom. It's as if it drops completely off the edge of the world! A gust of hot air hits my face as I peer down at the rising steam and smoke. The updraft carries with it the sound of voices… voices in agony… an unfathomable number of voices! What is this place? I wonder…then, I think I know.

I back away from the edge, shaking… afraid somehow I'll lose my footing, or the ground will crumble beneath me and I'll be lost in the abyss below.

I look over at the roadhouse, noticing that the back side of the building is hanging over the edge of the cliff, and that the front has started to lift off the ground! It could topple over the edge at any second! Maybe I should warn the people inside… But how? I can't risk entering the building!

As I stand there, trying to figure out what I should do, two men walk up to me on their way into the roadhouse.

"Hey! How's it going?" One of them asks me, as he slings his arm around his friend.

"Ummm… well… not too great, to be honest." I say awkwardly.

"Well, you should come on in to Dirty's Roadhouse! He makes the most delectable food around, and the drinks are great, too!" The other man says in a softer voice and bright, smiling teeth that appear too large for his face.

"We're regular customers." The first man says, grinning fondly at his fellow.

They seem to be REALLY friendly with each other… Probably partners. I feel awkward as I try to figure out how to warn them about the precarious situation of their favorite establishment…

"You know that building is hanging over the edge of the cliff over there, don't you?" I ask.

They look a little taken aback.

"Awww… It's been like that for years! If it was going to fall, it would have fallen long ago!" The first man answers.

"Come on, don't be such a worry wart!" Says the softer one, patting me on the back.

Edge of Eternity

They saunter into the roadhouse, laughing and elbowing each other playfully. I know better than to follow them, as tempting as a hot meal and a cup of coffee sounds...

I turn my back to the roadhouse and notice for the first time, a little vendor on the opposite side of the path. The sign above the stand reads, "Bread of Life, Free to all." I don't even have to step off the path to approach the stand, it sits right alongside it. I can't believe I hadn't noticed it before! A petite, older woman sits on a bench inside the little stand, she smiles as I step up to the counter.

"Hi, can I please have some bread?" I ask, feeling embarrassed. I've never been to a food stand that didn't expect payment... I feel like a bum!

"Of course! Here..." She pulls out a perfect little loaf of bread with a currant cross adorning the top.

"Can I pay you something for this?" I ask, even though I don't have a penny on me... I keep thinking there must be a catch of some sort...nothing's free, right?

"No, your meal has already been paid for." She says with a smile, "All you have to do is accept it. It will sustain you for the rest of your journey."

"Thank you..." I say accepting the loaf gladly.

"Thank the One who paid for you..." She says, and points to the little cross on the loaf.

"Ok..." I say, turning back to the path.

Suddenly, the ground shakes beneath my feet and there's a loud rumbling and cracking sound behind me! I spin around to face the roadhouse, just in time to see it tip up on its side, and topple over the edge of the cliff! The screams of the people inside echo in my ears as they fall, and grow fainter and fainter...

Oh, no! All of those people! Maybe I should have done more to warn them! I stand there in shock, trying to figure out what this means!

Then, my guardian appears, he's standing next to me, staring at the empty space where the roadhouse once stood.

"Should I have done more? Is this my fault?" I ask him, a lump in my throat.

"You did warn them. The choice to continue indulging in sinful pleasures was their own." He answers coldly.

"But...they didn't even know that what they were doing was wrong!" I protest, feeling their punishment was unfair.

"God's laws are written on the tables of every heart. They chose to ignore the tug of guilt, and continue in their wickedness." He states.

"I see..." I say, realizing how many times I'd felt that subtle tug, and chosen to dismiss it.

My angel disappears, and I decide to say a quick prayer of thanks as I walk. Something I haven't done in a long time. My prayer finished, I begin to munch on the bread, and feel my strength revive more with every bite.

The mid-morning sun hits an object along the path that reflects its light in a brilliant glare, nearly blinding me! I use my hand to shield my eyes as I approach whatever the source of the glare is. Gradually, I realize the light is reflecting off of a massive building, built right on top of the path, and covered on the outside with mirrors!

A house of mirrors... I swallow hard, anticipating what I might see inside. When I reach the front door of the building, I am greeted by a stout little man in a green silk waistcoat and matching pants.

"Welcome, to the House of Reflection!" He greets me, and without further ado, opens the door and waves me inside with a graceful gesture of his hand.

I have to smile at his mannerisms, like something from an old book or movie... but my smile disappears as I find myself standing in a massive foyer covered from ceiling to floor in mirrors! Reflections of myself dance around on every side, copying every move I make! It makes me feel dizzy, and I can hardly keep walking without teetering over. There must be thousands of mirrors in here!

There's only one way to go, although the room is massive, there is a lone door at the far side of it. The door is the only thing in this room not covered in reflective material, so I make my way toward it, trying to keep my eyes focused on it alone. As I reach the door, I take a deep breath, and turn the knob...

The heavy wooden door swings open slowly on its own, and a large, carpeted hallway stretches out in front of me. The walls on both sides are lined with mirrors in elegant frames, like portraits. I approach the first one and stare at my reflection in it. To my surprise, my fifteen-year-old self stares back at me and then turns to face something out of my field of vision. I watch, mesmerized as she smiles and greets someone...who is it? I let out a little gasp as I recognize my old friend Cassandra, from school. I feel a weight in the pit of my stomach as I watch them sit down on a park bench, and begin a conversation I had nearly forgotten took place...

"Emily...I don't know what to do. I'm pregnant. I can't let my parents find out! They'll be so disappointed..." She says, tears filling the corners of her eyes. "I just want this all to go away." She states, lip trembling.

"You have to do what's best for you." I hear myself telling her, putting my hand on her shoulder.

"You won't ever tell anyone?" She asks pleadingly.

"Of course not. You can trust me." I tell her, giving her a hug.

She thanks the younger me, gets up, and walks out of the field of vision. But the reflection of myself turns to me, a blank look on her face, and holds up her hands that are dripping with blood!

I recoil in horror! That didn't happen in real life! Then I let the realization of what it means sink in... Cassandra terminated her pregnancy shortly after that. I was partly to blame! I influenced her decision to take her baby's life. I never really thought about the baby, just what trouble it would cause for her...

"All life is precious to the Creator..." I turn to see my Guardian, standing next to me, peering sadly at the mirror on the wall.

"But, she hadn't been pregnant for very long..." I stammer, trying to defend myself, "The baby wasn't even viable yet."

Edge of Eternity

"Yet her eternal soul had been given to her, the moment she was conceived. She was no less alive to God than you are." He answers, not raising his voice, but his eyes flash with indignation.

"I'm sorry, I didn't realize..." I say, turning back to the mirror, which now simply reflects my face. "I wish I could..." But the angel is gone, and I'm once again alone in the hallway.

I turn to face the mirror on the opposite wall, not sure what I'm going to encounter this time. The image shows a little girl, maybe five-years-old. Me, again... She's sitting in Sunday school, singing about Jesus... She looks so happy! Her eyes shine brightly and her face radiates childish innocence. What happened to me? When did I forget that kind of joy and trust in things unseen?

Although I remember enjoying Sunday school, and the activities, I never really made the Faith my own. I never made that commitment to God, never accepted Christ as my personal Savior, though I heard the alter call many times growing up. I supposed that going to church with my parents was good enough. Something held me back from fully giving myself over to God. What WAS holding me back? I'm not really sure.

As I watch the little me in the mirror, something startling appears in the image. It's a creature, a dark creature, a sinister shadow... he sits behind me, leaning over my shoulder. As the teacher tries to explain the lesson, he covers my ears, or whispers some distraction that causes me to lose attention. Is this what really went on? The little girl seems to have no idea that the creepy entity is there! I watch her giggle and wiggle and then the image fades away. Hmmm...

I walk a few paces down the hallway and peer into the next mirror, adorned with a golden frame. In the image, I see my grandmother, before she passed away. She is sitting with me in the living room working on crocheting a doily for somebody's Christmas stocking. I was thirteen at the time, and I remember it well as it was the last conversation we had together before she died. She was trying to reach me - she knew I wasn't on a Christian path, and she had taken it upon herself this day to try and appeal to me. I remember how annoyed I was with her! I watch sadly as I roll my eyes, and see for the first time the pain in my grandmother's eyes as my rebellious, teenage self lets every word of wisdom roll off my back and into oblivion.

"Just leave me alone!" I finally say to her, getting up and stomping out of the room.

The image fades, and for the first time, I feel ashamed for how I treated her. If I had known that would be the last time I saw her, I would have acted differently... I wish I could do that day over again! I miss my grandma. She was a good woman, and she loved me dearly.

I feel a lump in my throat as I turn and walk down the hallway, stopping at the next mirror... dreading what might appear in its surface! This mirror, again, is a picture of my past, another of my mistakes... It is me and my very first boyfriend. The guy who seemed so perfect, and then turned out to be a great, big, jerk! I was so "in love" with him, I would have done anything for him! And when he asked me to give myself entirely to him, I did. I thought he loved me, too. But he really only wanted to take away my innocence... to be the first to do so. I blush as I watch the scenario begin to play out, and then turn away. I can't bear to go through that again! One of the most shameful nights of my life! After that, he stopped answering my texts, ignored my calls, and eventually I found out that he had moved on to his next conquest. What I thought would bring us closer together, only proved that he never had any real feelings for me. I'd wasted my virginity on a guy who didn't even care! It still makes me so angry!

I whirl around and grab the mirror, jerking it off the wall, and slam it face-down on the floor! It shatters in a thousand pieces! I notice that one of the larger shards still contains his disgusting, leering face! I stomp on it, grinding it hard with my heel until I feel it crunch under the pressure!

I'm done looking at mirrors! I ignore the other mirrors and tromp down the hallway to the door at the far end. Without pausing I turn the handle, yank the door open and smack head first into a mirror blocking my path! I stumble back rubbing my throbbing head and feeling a little dazed. Then, I confront the image in front of me, shrinking back as I see its horrible reflection grinning back at me!

The image is of me, but I am a hideous, zombie-like creature! My flesh and skin are rotting and falling off, revealing patches of skull and bones. The teeth grin at me, and the eyes stare at me in non-recognition! I scream as the zombie-me reaches through the mirror, grasping me by the throat with its icy fingers! How can this be? None of the other images could touch me!

I cry out for help, struggling futilely to pry the vice-like fingers off my neck! I feel the world begin to fade... darkness begins to creep into the corners of my vision...

"Please, God, help me..." I gurgle out the words, surprising myself!

Suddenly, my angel appears, I plead with him for help with my bulging eyes! He waves his hand and the zombie disappears! I crumple to the ground, choking and gasping for breath! When I regain myself enough to speak, I ask the angel why this image could touch me when the others could not.

"Because, Child of man, this image is you...as you truly are. The others were only memories of your past, of the choices you've made. This image is a reflection of the state of your soul." He says solemnly.

"But... in the reflection, I was dead!" I say aghast!

"Yes..." he answers, looking at me like I should understand.

"Sin brings death, spiritual death." He explains.

I swallow hard. So, all of these mirrors reflect the sins of my past... I peer down the long hallway, and at the many mirrors I didn't even look into.

"Is it too late? Can I still be saved?" I ask, feeling desperate.

"As long as you are alive, there is hope." He answers, "Continue on the path, there is only one way to attain salvation."

And he vanishes again. The mirror blocking my path shatters on its own, revealing the open air of the outdoors, and the path stretching out again in front of me.

Chapter 5: Innocence Lost

Soon, the path leaves the open plain and leads me through a narrow canyon. Boulders lie here and there on the path and now and then the crack of stone echoes around me as another is loosed from above and crashes to the ground! I look back towards the house of reflection and watch as the black wall closes in behind me, blocking it from view.

I'm left to continue down the narrow corridor, ducking and cringing every time I hear the crack of stone or the crash of a boulder! Then I hear something... a voice. It sounds like a child singing! I pick my way down the path a little faster, hopping and climbing over boulders and rubble. The voice gets louder and clearer as I go. It's a little girl's voice, singing a song I used to sing often as a child...

"Jesus loves me, this I know,

for the Bible tells me so.

Little ones to Him belong.

They are weak but He is strong."

I stop short when I notice the voice is now behind me. I spin around to see a little girl, sitting in the dirt behind a huge boulder and playing with a raggedy doll. She smiles as she sees me. I stand there a moment, trying to figure out what I'm supposed to say or do.

"Hi!" she says sweetly.

"Hi." I reply, kneeling down beside her, studying her round face.

For some reason, I think I know her... then I realize she looks a lot like my sister Kay did when she was little.

"What are you doing out here all alone?" I ask her, feeling concerned as I look around at the unstable walls of the canyon.

"I don't know. I guess I got lost." She answers, her round face growing serious.

"Come with me - let's get out of this place. It isn't safe." I say to her, holding out my hand which she readily accepts.

She trots alongside me, humming to herself. She doesn't seem to be troubled by the danger around her. She is just happy to hold my hand, and once in a while she kisses or speaks softly to her little doll.

"My name's Emily," I introduce myself, "What's yours?"

"Innocence." She says, almost too quiet for me to hear.

"Another interesting name..." I mumble to myself, looking curiously at her.

Now, I think I can see the end of the canyon! The sliver of pale light grows larger and larger as we continue our trek. I notice that the canyon has grown completely quiet, except for Innocence's gentle humming. Not a single pebble moves above us until we exit the crevice and the black wall closes behind us.

We step out into a forest clearing. It's not very large, maybe a hundred yards across, and is surrounded by tall, looming pine trees that sway and whisper in the midday breeze. It must be about noon, as the sun is almost directly overhead. My time here is half over... I don't feel like I've accomplished anything great yet!

Dead pine needles rustle under our feet as we cross the clearing. Occasionally, Innocence stomps on a pinecone, giggling at the crunching sound that it makes. I don't pay much attention to it, until a sound somewhere in the trees catches my ear. It sounds like a snarl...like that of a large dog... Then it howls... a long, blood curdling sound that I've only heard before on television! I feel like my heart might leap right out of my chest!

"What's that, Emily?" Innocence asks, tugging on my arm.

I look down at her small face. I don't want to scare her, but I don't know how to comfort her either!

"I don't know..." I say pulling her closer to me to shield her from whatever might come.

Then I see them, flitting figures moving through the trees... weaving their way closer and closer... Wolves! There are at least a dozen of them and they're enormous! Much larger than any natural wolf, these appear to be the size of horses! They stop at the tree line, peering out at us with eyes that glow with a yellow light. One of them lets out another piercing howl!

For several minutes, we stand like this, Innocence and I barely daring to breathe. I expect them to charge us at any moment and rip us to pieces! But they just stand there, staring, panting, and licking their chops... they don't venture a single step beyond the tree-line. I look at the path cutting through the trees, straight as an arrow as always. The wolves do not approach the path... I venture a couple of steps along it, and the wolves' growl and show their teeth, with their hackles standing on end! But they hold their ground.

Then, one of them approaches as close to the path as it dares... It whimpers at me, and dances around playfully, wagging its bushy tail. He appears to be the alpha male, and I'm confused by this change in his mannerisms. He pants at me, his sharp teeth forming a friendly grin. Then he sits as if waiting for me to come and pet him. The other wolves in the trees sit also, as if on cue. Their menacing appearance is gone, and I feel strangely drawn to them.

I lead Innocence by the hand and we enter the tree-line, keeping in the center of the path. The alpha sits within arm's reach, whining and wagging his tail. I stop, and look into his amber eyes that glow unnaturally. I feel torn inside, something compels me to reach out to him, and something else urges me to keep going...

The wolf's steady gaze draws me in like a magical spell...and I find my hand reaching out involuntarily, nearly touching the wet tip of his nose! My hand trembles as the battle to stay, and the battle to go wages inside me...

Then, suddenly, the wolf's countenance changes again, and his eyes betray the hatred in his heart as he makes a sudden snap for my hand! I recoil just in time as his jaws snap shut on the empty space where my hand was!

What was I thinking? I wonder to myself as I urge Innocence to stay in the center of the path! I can't believe I almost fell for that! A fraction of a second, and he would have dragged me off of the path and the pack would have devoured me! That was close, Emily! Too close...

The wolves snarl and snap and pace back and forth along the sides of the path, but they cannot touch us! My heart is still pounding as we continue along the path, careful not to step a single foot off of its protective boundary! I wish it wasn't so narrow! Sometimes it's no wider than a balance beam and we must carefully place each step.

The tall pines eventually open up into another clearing, and I pull the little girl faster along the path, eager to get away from these dreadful creatures!

All the wolves howl and bark and growl, and I glance behind me just in time to see the alpha male leap towards me, teeth barred and claws ready to rip me to shreds! I scream and hunker down on the path, doing my best to shield Innocence!

I hear a loud yelp as the wolf seems to bounce off an invisible barrier! I stand up and watch as he gives me a menacing glare, and then saunters off, tail tucked beneath him. He disappears into the trees, followed by the rest of the pack, and I breathe a sigh of relief.

I am startled as I turn around and see my angel standing directly in front of me!

"What were those creatures?" I ask him.

"They are the company of the wicked - you used to be a part of them." He answers.

I ponder this for a moment...

"You mean my friends?" I ask, surprised.

"The wrong friends will lead you away from God." He answers, and then is gone.

We continue down the path, which cuts through another small wooded area and then enters a great, open plain with a massive city situated at its center. On the left side of the path is a paved road running parallel to it. Next to the road sits a red sports car, whose driver leans against the driver's side door as if he's waiting for something. He's tall with dark hair and wears a red, polo shirt that matches the shade of his car. He smiles as he spots us.

"Hey!" he calls, beckoning to us with his hand.

I pause, not sure what to do. So far, leaving the path has been a big "no-no," so I should probably just ignore this guy... I pretend not to notice him, and continue on the path with Innocence trailing behind me.

"Wait!" he yells, running to catch up to us.

I pause on the path. I guess if he's going to come over here, it couldn't hurt to talk to him...

He's a little out of breath as he reaches us. I study him as he takes a second to catch his breath before speaking. He's very handsome, and has stunning black eyes that twinkle in an enchanting way...

"Hi, I'm Tem," he introduces himself cheerfully. "I live in the City of Acceptance, over there," he points to the city and continues. "It's several miles' walk to the city. Would you like a ride?"

His twinkling eyes and kind smile seem sincere, and he doesn't appear dangerous... I glance at the path that also leads directly to the city. Since he's going to the same place, and time is limited... it couldn't hurt to take him up on his offer, could it?

"Mommy says not to take rides from strangers." Innocence says shyly, tugging on my arm.

"Your mommy also let you play in a canyon with crashing boulders, and walk through woods filled with wolves." I say, feeling annoyed.

"Come on… we're all friends here." Says Tem, smiling down at the little girl who slides behind me and glares at him.

"It'll be ok." I assure Innocence, "I'll take care of you."

She looks at me a little bewildered, but doesn't argue any more. We follow Tem over to the car and I buckle Innocence into the front seat with me.

"Hold on!" Tem says with a grin and revs the engine loudly. The car peels out on the pavement and we speed along the flat, straight stretch of road!

I feel a little apprehensive about my decision to accept this ride now. We're flying down the road, and I notice the path out my window getting a little further and further off to the side as we go.

"So, you want to see some of the best places in town?" Tem asks me with a smile.

"I'm kind of in a hurry…otherwise I'd love to." I answer, feeling the weight of my impending death heavy on my mind.

"Aww… come on! At least let me buy you a coffee or something. You look like you could use a break." He says persuasively.

It's hard to resist his warm smile and dark eyes…

"Well, I guess…" I say hesitantly.

"Do you want a smoothie or something?" I ask Innocence beside me.

She doesn't answer, but just stares out the window. She must be upset with me. As we approach the city, it looms up above us with its tall skyscrapers and towers. A dark haze seems to hang in the air over it, dimming the light of the sun… Smog, I guess.

I look out the window and realize the straight path is completely out of sight! Oh, no! I need to find it again, and fast!

"Stumble off the path, and I will take you sooner…" the words of Justice spring back into my mind.

I feel like I'm having a panic attack! There's no way I'm going to let Justice catch up to me!

I look over at Tem who has just put on a pair of dark sunglasses with the words, "No Evil" written on the front of them. How can he see well enough to drive with words right in front of his eyes like that? He's still driving recklessly as we enter the city's traffic.

"I need to get back to the path!" I blurt out, unable to hide the concern in my voice.

"Sure, I'll take you there. Right after I show you the sights." He says, smiling reassuringly.

"No, I don't have time for that! I need to get back there, now!" I shout frantically. He lowers his sunglasses and gives me a startled look.

"Watch out!" I scream, as he nearly runs over an old woman on a cross-walk!

The car swerves and spins out of control, crashing into another vehicle! I hit my head on the dashboard, and everything goes black...

My ears are ringing... Gradually, my eyes come back into focus and I survey the damage around me.

Innocence! Where is she? The windshield is completely smashed, and the passenger door is open beside me. Other than the ringing in my ears, I seem to be unharmed. I hear angry voices, shouting and cursing as I step out of the car.

"It was her fault!" Tem's voice rings out. "She made me wreck - she's crazy!" His eyes flash with rage as they meet mine.

There are police lights flashing all around me, and officers are taking pictures of Tem's totaled sports car and of the other vehicle involved, which is also in poor shape.

Where is Innocence? I scan the area, looking for an ambulance or something, but no one seems to have called for one. She must be ok...

Then I see her, a crumpled little figure, lying on the ground!

"Innocence!" I scream, rushing over to her and scooping her up in my arms.

"Somebody help her!" I cry out, looking at the officers standing by, and the crowd gathered around Tem, who's still yelling and pointing at me.

A few people look at me in disgust, but no one comes to the aid of the little girl lying unconscious in my arms.

"Innocence, can you hear me?" I ask, brushing the hair out of her pale face.

She doesn't move, or make a sound...not even a breath. I press my ear to her chest and listen for a heartbeat... nothing.

"Oh, no! What have I done?" I cry, sobbing uncontrollably. "I told you it would be ok!" I bawl, sitting on the ground, cradling her lifeless body.

"I'm sorry! I'm so sorry! Please, Lord, help me! I'm so, so sorry!" I cry, as I rock the little girl, praying and hoping that somehow God can forgive me, and undo the terrible thing I've done. Then I feel a gentle hand on my shoulder and look up to see my angel standing there with a curious look on his face.

"It was an accident! I didn't meant for this to happen!" I wail.

"You were warned not to leave the path..." he says gravely.

I start to defend myself, but realize there's no use. I left the path, I knew better.

"Please, I know this is my fault. But can't you fix this? Can't you bring her back?" He looks down at the child in my arms and scoops her up into his own.

"Innocence, once lost, can never be brought back, Child of man. Now you feel the impact of her loss, as the death of this child." He looks sadly at the limp figure in his arms.

"I..." but I don't know what to say.

He doesn't speak again, he just turns and disappears into thin air, and they are gone.

Chapter 6: The Truth Shall Set You Free

A police officer approaches me. He looks angry.

"Miss, put your hands behind your back!" he commands.

"What? Why am I being arrested? It was just an accident!" I protest, as he roughly handcuffs my hands behind my back with a grunt.

"You're being arrested for deliberate destruction of Mr. Temptation's personal property, endangering his safety, and the safety of the citizens of The City of Acceptance." He says as he leads me towards a police car.

"I didn't do it on purpose, it was just an accident." I protest again, though I can see it's useless.

I am shoved into the back of the car without another word. I glance out the window to see Tem scowl at me as the car pulls away. We pull up in front of the city's police department and I am escorted inside. The officer checks me in at the desk and then marches me straight back to a jail cell, slamming the door as he shoves me in.

This is not good. I'm running out of time, and now I'm stuck in here! I spy a clock on the far wall...3:15. It's summer, so hopefully it won't get dark until after 8:00. I need to get out of here! I look over at the cell next to me which is occupied by a small, frail woman, whose eyes appear to be much too large for her face.

"Are you ok?" She asks me quietly.

"I don't know." I answer, crossing my arms and trying unsuccessfully not to cry.

The woman waits patiently while I sit on the bench and sob my heart out. When I regain my composure, I look over at her, and realize how terribly sick she looks. Her cheekbones jut out of her pale face, and her arms are so thin her elbows look like knobs on a stick. Her ribcage and backbone shows clearly through her tank top which is stained and worn. Her dark, curly hair is streaked with white, though she doesn't appear to be older than thirty.

"Are YOU ok?" I ask her.

"No, but I will be...soon." She answers with a far off look in her eye.

"What's wrong with you? Why are you so frail, and sick?" I ask, guessing she must have done drugs or something to damage her body so.

"I'm starving. I've been left in here to die." She says flatly.

"What? They can't do that! There are laws against that!" I say, barely believing her.

"Not here..." She replies sadly.

"Why have they done this to you?" I ask, anger welling up inside me.

"For speaking the truth... in fact, that is my name, Truth." She replies, as she sits down on the bench close to the bars dividing our cells.

"I don't understand. Isn't there freedom of speech here?"

"Yes," she answers, "But only if what you say doesn't conflict with the views of the townspeople. If you tell them that what they see as freedom or pleasure is wrong, then they lock you away and you are never heard from again. My sisters have already died here, their names were Purity, and Righteousness. Here, you are free to do anything that you please, except stand for what's right, or against what's wrong."

"But how do you know what's right, or wrong? Isn't what's right for each person different? Aside from harming someone else, the lifestyle you choose is irrelevant, right?" I ask, as this was my general understanding.

"Sin is sin, it doesn't matter how it's presented. If it's presented as just an alternative lifestyle, it makes it no less a sin, if it's presented as a person's right to choose, it's still a sin. God's laws don't change. Acceptance of sin is Satan's newest and greatest weapon! If he can make people no longer see sin as something wrong, if he can get them to accept it as just another way of living, then countless souls will be lost to destruction. They are being lost even as we speak." She says sadly.

"So you are in here dying, because you don't want those around you lost to sin? Even though they don't want to listen to you? Why die for them? They don't deserve it!" I ask her, looking into her deep, brown eyes.

"Because..." she says softly, "My Savior did so for me."

"But if He loves you, why would He want you to throw away your life like this?" I ask, feeling frustrated.

"I'm not throwing my life away, I'm laying it down. All I have to do to leave here is to admit to the judge that what I said was wrong, and they will let me go free. But I can't. If my words can reach one single soul, and save it from hell, then it is worth laying down my life, many times over." She says, appearing weaker and weaker as we speak.

"No, you can't die like this! This is ridiculous!" I storm over to the door of my cell and spy a deputy sitting near the door to the office.

"Hey! This woman needs help! She needs a doctor!" I yell at him.

He just sits there, playing on an Ipad or something, I can't tell for sure. He doesn't even look up. He must not have heard me!

"HEY! OVER HERE!" I yell louder, rattling the cell door.

"Deputy Callous… doesn't hear or see the suffering of those in his charge. He won't help. Soon, I will receive my freedom. You, Emily, will have to free yourself." Truth says as she points to an inscription above the door of my cell.

"The truth shall set you free." It reads.

"What truth? The truth about what?" I ask, feeling baffled.

I turn to her, she gives me a weak smile and then closes her eyes.

"I don't know what you mean! Please, tell me what you mean!" I scream at her, hoping she'll wake up!

But she doesn't. She never speaks again. I'm left here alone, except for Deputy Callous, who may as well not be here. I study the inscription over the door again, and then notice for the first time, the locking system on the door. It's very sophisticated! There are six locks intermittent on the side of the door. They are all wired to a box with a little flashing light on it. Right now the light is yellow.

It appears to have a microphone on it, I test it out… "Hello?" The little light flashes green, then turns red.

"Hmmm… George Washington was the first president of the United States - that's true!" I say into the box.

Red light.

I think hard. What does it want me to say? Considering where I'm at, I suppose it must be something about myself.

"My name is Emily. I'm nineteen years old, and I'm dying. I have been dying for some time now. I just didn't know it."

Green light, click! One of the locks is open! Let's see… what else have I learned today?

"I thought I was a decent person. I thought that since others were doing the same things, that it couldn't be wrong for me to do them. But it was."

Green light, another lock clicks open.

I think for a while… trying to sort through the events that have taken place in this strange, dream-world…

"I allowed myself to be led away from God by temptation, and have lost my innocence."

Click…

"I haven't shown love or compassion to those around me."

Green light, click…

I try a couple of trivial admissions about things in my past, but the light flashes red. I admit to stealing part of my mother's grocery money to buy earrings, to kissing another boy at a party while dating Chase, to pretending to say my prayers at night while thinking about other things… What does it want?

An agonizing half-hour of guessing passes… and still the light flashes red! I bang my forehead against the bars of the cell-door, there's something I haven't admitted yet, but what?!

"I deserve to be punished for the things I have done."

Click!

Yes! Only one lock left! I dig down deep into my heart and soul, squeezing my eyes shut as I search for the final answer… I'm drawing a blank! Come on, Emily! Think! Then, I say a silent prayer - a prayer for guidance, and it's as if a small voice gently speaks to my heart in words so clear it nearly brings me to tears.

I swallow the lump in my throat as conviction floods over me and the weight of my past sins sink in.

"I am unworthy of eternal life, I need forgiveness."

Click! And the door swings loose on the hinges!

That was surprisingly easy, and yet surprisingly hard. I quietly creep past the deputy and out the door. He never once looks up from what he's doing. I exit the sheriff's office, doing my best to appear calm, and casual.

Edge of Eternity

No one questions me as I turn a corner, and breathe deeply the heavy, city air! Freedom! Now to find my way back to the straight path! I have no idea which direction to go, I'm all turned around.

I study the surrounding buildings, this area appears to be old. Many of the buildings are made of brick, and have old advertisements painted on them that are faded and chipping away. The streets are littered with trash and the people who pass me on the sidewalks peer at me suspiciously over their tinted sunglasses, the words, "No Evil" printed on every pair.

As I walk along, I realize how few children I have seen the entire time I've been here… I wonder if some sickness or calamity may be responsible. The thought makes me sad. Finally, I approach a young woman, sitting on a bench near a small park. She is looking at her heavily made up face in a small, pocket mirror. Her platinum hair is pulled up into a stylish knot of ringlets that cascade from beneath her felt hat adorned with bright feathers and black netting. She has a small, fluffy dog on her lap, her clothes are very fine, and she is wearing high heels so tall I suspect she would break an ankle if she were to misstep.

"Excuse me…" I say politely. She peers over her sunglasses, looking surprised. "Could I ask you a couple of questions?"

"Are you a reporter?" She asks, her ruby painted lips spread into a dazzling smile, revealing her unnaturally white teeth.

"Uh…no. I was wondering if you could point me in the direction of the straight path? It cuts through this city, and I really need to find it."

Her smile is instantly replaced by a frown, "Why would you want to find that? It's a blight on our beautiful city! Only ignorant, superstitious people travel on it! You must be one of them…" She rolls her eyes and turns her head away.

"Can you at least point me in the general direction?" I ask, feeling disgusted.

"No, I really can't. I'm not good with directions. I go wherever suits me best, I don't care which 'direction' as long as it's enjoyable!" she says with her nose pointed up in the air.

"Don't you get lost?" I ask, giving in to the urge to annoy her a bit.

"Hmmph! Lost? Who cares about lost? I can find something to please me most anywhere." She says, snippily.

"But don't you wish you knew where you belonged? Don't you have a family or a home? Someone who loves you?" I ask, beginning to feel sorry for her, even though she disgusts me.

"Just leave me alone! I have plenty of people who 'love' me! I can find someone to love me whenever I want! Any day or night of the week!" she practically shrieks!

"That's not real love." I say, and walk away, leaving her to figure that out for herself.

I come to a busy intersection and read the signs above. One says "Please Yourself Street" the other says "All Is Well Avenue." I pause here, not sure which way to go. I see a couple coming up to the crosswalk, where they press the button and wait for the "Walk" signal to turn on. I watch them for a second, wondering if maybe they might give me directions...

They are both young, about my age. The girl is short, and has hazel eyes just a little darker than her honey colored hair. She looks sad, dark circles cradle her eyes and she appears haggard and worn beyond her years. The guy is tall, muscular, and handsome. He seems to be in fine health, unlike the girl, and stands over her, a hand on her shoulder in a possessive way. The "Walk" sign comes on and the guy gives the girl a shove, which causes her to stumble and fall into the street!

"What's wrong with you!?" He screams at her, "Are you trying to embarrass me? Get up!" and he jerks her roughly to her feet by the back of her neck.

"I'm sorry! I tripped!" She cries, cowering as if waiting for a blow.

"Now we don't have time to cross! We'll have to wait again. Why are you such a klutz?" He glares at her gripping her shoulder so hard his knuckles turn white.

"I'm sorry..." she says quietly, her lower lip trembles and I can tell she's struggling to hold back tears.

Then he raises his free hand, as if to slap her, and I can't contain my anger anymore! I know I probably shouldn't, but I march right up to the brute and rip his hand off of her!

"How about you back off and leave her alone!" I yell at him, scowling into his face.

He looks at me, with wide eyes, as if he's never been challenged before in his life! Then his eyes become angry slits, and his face turns red and contorts with fury...

"Who do YOU think you are?" he asks, voice shrill with rage.

"It doesn't matter, you just leave her alone!" I put myself between him and her and stare him down, every muscle in my body is rigid, and I can hear my heart pounding in my ears.

"Whatever!" he screams at me.

He casts the girl a shriveling glance as the light changes and he storms off across the intersection alone.

"Why did you do that?" the girl asks me quietly.

"No one should treat another person like that!" I say, feeling shaky now that the confrontation is over. "Why do you stay with a creep like that?"

She shrugs, and stares at her feet, "He's my boyfriend, and I love him. I don't know how to leave him."

"How can you love someone like that?" I ask, feeling aggravated.

"Because, Sin is the only guy who's ever taken an interest in me. I'll be all alone if I leave him. I'm afraid no one else will love me." She says sadly.

"But he DOESN'T love you! You don't treat someone you love like that!" I say catching sight of him leaning against the side of a building on the other side of the street, waiting for her to follow.

"Come with me instead - I'm searching for Someone who has already shown us true love, Someone who loved us so much, He died for us." I practically plead with her.

"Who is this person, and why are you searching for Him if He's already dead?" She asks, looking puzzled.

"Jesus, He died to take our sins away, but He rose again, and now He lives forever! He has conquered death so we can live with Him! I'm searching for Him, I need His forgiveness... I need freedom from sin, too." I say quietly.

She bites her lip, and casts a glance across at her boyfriend, who jerks his head for her to come to him.

"I don't know...." She wavers, then clenches her jaw tightly. "Yes... I am ready to be free." She says, waving goodbye to her beau, who stomps his foot and waves his fist in anger!

I can hear him screaming her name as he parallels our path on the other side of the street, "Helpless, you can't leave me! There's no one who can take care of you better than me!" He shrieks at her.

"Yes, there is." She calls back. "This girl... what's your name?" She asks, turning to me.

"Emily." I answer.

"Emily says there is Someone who loves me, and can free me from you!" she yells over at him.

"Helpless, I'm sorry! I can do better, I promise! Please, come home with me!" He pleads with her now with desperation in his voice.

"No, Sin... it's over." She calls back, turning away from him and never looking back despite his desperate pleas.

She looks at me and smiles. I smile back, and then remember... I don't know where the path is!

"Do you know the way to the straight path from here?" I ask her.

"Of course! It's right near my house! I look at it out my window every day..." She answers, her voice trailing off as she realizes the answer to her troubles has been so close this whole time.

"Then, let's go! I'll follow you!" I say, feeling hopeful for the first time since I arrived in this awful place.

Helpless leads us on as we wind our way through the city. I'm very glad that she knows where we're going - I'd be lost here for hours!

"So, I haven't seen many kids around, why is that?" I ask Helpless as we walk.

She looks a little sad as she answers, "Nobody wants them. Children put a damper on the easy lifestyle prized by the people here. They are either placed in boarding schools at an early age, or never allowed to be born in the first place."

"I see..." I say, thinking again of my friend Cassandra.

The longer I walk through this city, the more I hate it, and the hard-heartedness of its residents! How can people live like this? Can they truly be happy? The answer is no... they are trying to fill an emptiness in their souls with temporary pleasures. But they can't succeed... it's a hole that only God and His love can fill. They'll never feel true love or happiness while the hole remains, but the things they try to fill it with only make them more empty. It's tragic... Then I realize it was my life, too...

We walk quietly through the rest of the city. I have a lot to process... As we finally reach the path, the sun is getting close to the horizon. There's only a couple of hours left before it sets.

"This is the way," I say, pointing down the path, "I need to travel fast, you can walk with me if you can keep up." I tell her.

"You go on ahead." She says with a smile, "I'll manage from here on my own."

"Safe travels!" I call back to her as I jog down the path, eager to get out of the city!

As I go, several townspeople call me names, or mock me, but I do my best to ignore them. They're the ones who are ridiculous, not me.

Finally, the open plain once again spreads out before me and a blast of fresh air hits my face! I spread my arms out like wings, letting the cool wind blow away the filth of the city that clings to me like an invisible cloak. I feel like I could run forever! My heart feels lighter than it has in years! I know that I'm on the right track. I know that I must make things right with my Creator. Now I just need to figure out how!

I run and run until my muscles finally can't keep up the pace anymore. My throat is parched with thirst, and I must walk slowly for a while to catch my breath. Shortly, I come to a sparkling pool of water. It's right next to the path, so I assume it's safe.

I'm so thirsty that I don't stop to read the sign next to the water's edge. Before I know it, my feet are stuck fast in the mud at the bank! I try to free them, but the more I struggle, the deeper I sink! Then I realize that I'm gradually sliding down into the water…it creeps up my ankles, and then up to my shins! I'm going to drown if I don't get out of here!

"Help! Somebody, help!" I cry out, trying futilely to pull my feet out of the mud again!

But no one shows up… the water is up to my knees, and I reach for the sign near the water's edge – the one I ignored a few moments ago. I grab hold of it and try to use it to pull myself out, but the sign comes loose and I lose my balance, falling backwards into the mud with a plop! Now, I'm up to my waist in mud and icy cold water! I stare at the wooden sign in my hands, "Pool of Discouragement" it reads…

I try to use the sign to paddle myself out of the mud, but it's useless.

"Help! Lord, why won't you help me!" I cry to the sky above, which is beginning to turn orange as the sun meets the hazy clouds near the top of the distant mountains.

But there is no answer… no one comes to my aid.

Then, on the other side of the pool, I see Justice. He stands there, waiting, arms folded, a look almost like sadness in his eyes…

waiting for the water to swallow me up. He shakes his head at me in apparent disappointment.

"I was going the right way! I didn't leave the path, this pool was right next to it! I didn't mean to fall in! Please, give me another chance!" I plead with him.

"Second chances are not mine to give." He answers, watching as the water creeps up to my chest.

Then, I pray in earnest, something I've never really done before! Before all of this, my prayers were just casual words of "thanks" or a request for help to some distant Deity. Now I beg Him, I beg Him to give me another chance, to forgive me for my mistake, to save me from the peril I find myself in! Then a strange voice catches my attention.

"Why are you doing that? Do you really think He cares about a sinner like you?" the smooth, melodic voice asks.

I glance around me, trying to figure out where the voice is coming from. Then I notice it, the reflection in the water that stares back up at me isn't mine! It's a woman's face, she has fine features and bold make-up that reminds me of an Egyptian queen! A faint smile appears on her ruby lips as she sees that I've noticed her.

"Yes, I believe He does!" I answer, teeth chattering as the water creeps up to my collar-bone.

"Then why doesn't He come and save you now?" she asks incredulously.

"I don't know..." I admit, feeling abandoned and scared.

"The answer is, because it's too late. You can't be saved. You may as well give in... Stop struggling. Accept your fate." She says with mock sympathy.

"No, I don't believe that." I protest, glancing around once more for something I might have missed!

"It's true... He doesn't really care for you. Why would He? Millions upon millions of pitiful human beings, and you think He could truly care for each one? Ridiculous! Face it, Emily... it's over! You're finished!" She laughs evilly as the water creeps up my neck - the chill makes me gasp!

I cry out, one last time, "Please, Heavenly Father, save me! I can't get out of here on my own!"

I flail around in desperation, and my hand brushes something just beneath the surface of the water! I catch hold of it tightly - it's a rope! A thick, strong rope! I grip it with both hands and pull with all of my strength, plunging head and all beneath the cold surface of the water in order to get enough leverage! Pain and shock envelopes my body as I pull and struggle in the liquid that entombs me in its icy grasp! I can't hold my breath much longer! I put every ounce of strength into my efforts to free myself!

Just in time, I feel the grip of the mud loosening from my feet and legs. My left foot pulls free and then my right! I pull and paddle myself to the water's edge sputtering and gasping for air! I stumble over and plant my feet firmly on the path - I will not step foot off of it again!

I stand there, dripping, and look across at Justice, who gives me an approving nod, and disappears.

Closing my eyes, I whisper "Thank you, God!"

Turning my attention back to the path in front of me, I see that it leads to a mountain in the distance. As I stare at it, it dawns on me that it's shaped like a gigantic skull, gazing back at me with hollow, cavernous eye-sockets... I shudder as I wonder what might await me there. But I am resolved to follow the path, no matter what perils loom ahead. And so I continue on, putting one foot in front of the other. I won't be discouraged, I won't give up.

Chapter 7: The Final Stretch

I plod steadily along, but appear to grow no closer to the mountain ahead of me. The path seems to grow longer and longer, and I watch with dismay as the sun touches the mountains, creating a fabulous, colorful display! Sunset, and I haven't reached my destination! Perhaps I'm not going to make it after all!

My heart sinks at the thought and I try to quicken my pace, but I'm too tired! In fact, I feel utterly exhausted! My struggle in the Pool of Discouragement wore me out, and I can barely put one foot in front of the other! All around me there is nothing but silence, not even the usual chirping of insects that accompanies the coming of evening. This silence seems to weigh me down, and I struggle even more to keep going. My eyelids droop and I yawn... but I can't stop here, there isn't time to rest!

The black wall that usually closes off the sections of my journey, now follows directly behind me. I can see it in my peripheral vision as I walk, and I know I must keep going. There is no other choice. Yet the path stretches on, and the silence is driving me crazy! I don't know how much longer I can take this monotony! The sun creeps lower and lower, already half concealed by the horizon. Then I see something - a small, white object, like a piece of paper, a couple hundred yards ahead of me.

Edge of Eternity

I quicken my pace, encouraged by the appearance of something new. The object grows closer, and closer, and at least I know I'm making progress. When I finally reach it, I see that it is, in fact, a piece of paper. I snatch it up, hoping it will contain some word of encouragement to speed me on my journey. But it doesn't. It's blank, silent... like the growing twilight around me. My heart falls and I feel a lump in my throat! I feel so utterly alone and helpless!

I fall to my knees and stare at the emptiness around me. All strength fails me, and I know I can't go on any further. The wall of blackness creeps steadily closer, threatening to crush me if I don't keep ahead of it.

Then, a voice, a gentle voice... calls my name, "Emily..."

It's coming from the mountain! I force myself back onto my feet, stumbling towards it. My knees wobble beneath me, and I pause, gripping my burning thighs.

The voice calls to me again, "Emily, come to me."

I force myself to take a step, and then another. The mountain that seemed so unattainable finally grows closer, and I step into its shadow in the fading light of the sun that is now only a sliver of light on the horizon.

Finally, I reach the base of the mountain. It looms ominously above me, like a sleeping monster that might awaken and devour me at any moment.

I force myself to climb... sometimes on my feet, sometimes on my hands and knees. But I keep going, following the voice that now and then calls my name, growing ever closer.

The path is treacherous, covered in sharp rocks that shift and slide beneath my feet and cut my hands or knees if I lose my footing and fall on them. It's getting dark now, there's just a pale strip of light above the mountains, the sky is purple, and the first stars are beginning to peek through the haze.

After what seems like an eternity, I reach the summit of the mountain. A cool gust of wind blows my hair over my eyes, and as I brush it away, I catch sight of the silhouette of a cross, standing alone at the edge of the plateau. It's still a fair distance away, maybe a quarter of a mile. I start making my way towards it, stumbling with fatigue even though the ground is more level now.

Then, I feel a presence near me, and turn to see Justice, standing a few yards away with a sword drawn in his hand.

"Emily, your time is up. Your blood must now be spilled for your wickedness, and your soul enter its punishment." He says coldly, holding the sword in front of him.

"No, wait! I've learned so much! I admit that there's a God, and that I'm a sinner! I know I've done wrong, and that I need to repent! I repent now! I'm sorry!" I wail, backing away from him.

He doesn't say anything, but walks steadily towards me.

"I need more time, just a little more time!" I cry, turning to run away.

Adrenaline surges through my veins giving a burst of energy to my worn out muscles!

I flee towards the cross, it's the only thing I can see in the growing darkness. I can hear the drag of Justice's chains closing in on me! With a final effort, I throw myself beneath the cross, falling on my hands and knees into a dark liquid beneath it...Blood!

Justice is right on top of me now, he raises his sword and I put up my blood covered hands to shield myself! But his blow falls short...

I stare up in astonishment as his countenance changes and he puts his sword back into the sheath at his side.

"Your debt... has been paid." He says and I think I see a faint smile on his face.

Then, all of what's taken place pieces itself together in my mind. Yes, I am a sinner, worthy of death. As much as I learned, and as hard as I tried to save myself, it is only by the blood that Christ shed for me that I can be spared from punishment!

"Thank you, Jesus!" I cry out, lifting my voice to heaven above, "Thank you for paying the price for my sins! For taking my punishment upon yourself! Thank you for being my Savior, and Lord of all! I give my heart, my soul, my life to you!"

Tears of joy stream down my cheeks. I made it! I found the answer I sought, and heaven will be my reward!

"Welcome to the Kingdom!" Justice says with an approving nod, and then disappears.

Then, my guardian angel appears, he is also smiling, and greets me warmly.

"Now, Child of God, there is one last thing you must do…"

"What's that?" I ask, feeling apprehensive.

"You already know." He answers.

Suddenly, the dream-world vanishes, and everything turns white and fuzzy… I gradually become aware of the steady beep of the heart monitor and quiet voices around me… I'm in my hospital room, back in the real world.

My eyes flutter open, and things come slowly into focus… I don't feel any pain. I look down at my limp hand that has an IV line taped to it, and see my feet there, beneath a hospital blanket. At my side I see my mother…dozing in a chair next to my bed!

"Mom?" I say, my voice sounds weak, even to me.

Her eyes fly open and she gasps!

"Emily! You're awake! Thank God! The doctors didn't think you'd ever speak again!"

"Mom, where's Chase?" I ask, scanning the room for his familiar, tall form.

"I'll call him!" She says, hastily pulling out her cell phone. "He just went home about an hour ago…" she explains as she waits for him to answer, "He's been here by your bedside for the last fourteen hours…"

"Oh, Chase!" She switches gears as he picks up on the other line, "Chase, she's awake! She's asking for you! Yes, come right away!" she hangs up and smiles at me.

"He's coming, Emily! He'll be here in fifteen minutes." She comes over and sits beside me on the hospital bed, lifting my limp hand and hugging it against her face.

I can't feel her hand grasp mine, I can't seem to feel anything. I try to move, but my neck is in a brace, and I don't seem to be able to move any part of my body...

"What happened to me? Is there anything broken?" I ask, dreading the answer.

Her face grows grave...

"Emily... I... I'm sorry. The doctor's say you've suffered a serious neck injury, and you have some bleeding on your brain. I don't know what the prognosis is. But you're awake, and that's a good sign, right?" she says with a weak smile.

"Sure, Mom..." I say smiling as best as I can.

But in my heart, I know...I'm not going to pull through this. I can feel it. Something deep down, tugs at me... another realm is calling me, pulling me away from this earthly existence. I cannot resist its call for much longer. But I hold on, willing myself to stay. I need to talk to Chase. I need to make things right.

A nurse comes in, takes my vitals, and asks me if I'm in any pain. I try to shake my head, "no" but realize I can't! I reassure her that there's no pain, and she leaves the room again. My mother strokes my hair and hums to me as we wait for the rest of my family and Chase to arrive.

"Emily, I love you so much!" My mom kisses my forehead and I smile at her.

"I love you, too." I whisper back.

I feel so tired...Finally, I hear voices coming toward my room, I recognize Kay's and my Dad's. They burst into the room, and Kay runs over and wraps me tightly in a hug! My mom pries her off, scolding her for being so rough.

"Emily, you're going to be ok now, right?" Kay asks expectantly.

"Sure, kiddo. I'm going to be ok." I smile at her.

She looks relieved and tells me how worried she's been, and that she didn't know what she'd do if I died. I glance over at my dad, who smiles at me, but he can't hide the sadness in his eyes. Kay may not know how grave my injuries are, but Dad does. Then, Chase enters the room followed by my brother.

"Emily! Emily, I'm so sorry!" Chase rushes over to me and grabs my hand, a pained sob escaping despite his efforts to keep it in check.

"Chase, it's not your fault." I say gently.

"But you wouldn't be here if it wasn't for me! I should have never taken you out there!" He says angrily, "It was stupid of me! Can you ever forgive me?" He asks with tears in his eyes.

"Chase... you did nothing wrong! In fact... you helped save me. You helped me realize what a dangerous path I was on...One that led to death. If it wasn't for you, I might not have realized that I needed to change, to make things right with God. I needed Jesus as my Savior, and now I've found Him."

I recount briefly to them my vision-journey and the things I learned about myself. And then I tell them about my new life, the one I have in Christ Jesus.

"Please, will you get the Chaplain, so he can pray with me?" I ask my father, who gladly rushes off at once.

When the Chaplain arrives, I pray with him the sinner's prayer of repentance and ask Jesus to be my personal Savior. My family rejoices with me, and Chase, moved by my change of heart, asks that the Chaplain pray with him, too.

My heart is so full of joy, it takes me a moment to realize that the happy, familiar faces around me are beginning to grow fuzzy... This world is fading away, and this time, I can't hold on to it anymore.

Suddenly, my eyes open, and I see things more clearly than I've ever seen them before. It takes me a second to figure out what's happened. Then I realize that I'm staring down at myself, my eyes are closed, my body at rest. The heart monitor is no longer beeping with the steady rhythm of my heartbeat, it's flat-lined and a flurry of doctors and nurses are frantically trying to revive the lifeless form of my past habitation. I'm transfixed by the commotion and drama that plays out as they finally realize their efforts are futile and there's no bringing me back. I don't feel sad, or scared. I just feel a strange awe as I realize my earthly toil is over, and eternity awaits me.

Then, I feel a gentle hand on my shoulder and see my angel standing next to me.

"Are you ready, Child of God?" he asks gently.

I look one last time at my mother as she sobs, clutching my body in her arms.

"I'll see you again, Mom." I call to her, knowing she can't hear me.

"Yes, I'm ready." I answer, taking his hand.

The End

About The Author

Shiree Walker lives with her husband, Brian and their three lovely children on their homestead in Eastern Washington. She has loved reading and writing since she was a child, and it has always been her dream to be an author. Besides writing, she enjoys the outdoors and loves to spend her time gardening, fishing, hunting, and gathering as the seasons permit. You can find her on Twitter, @ShireeWalker, and on Facebook at https://www.facebook.com/ShireesStories

Printed in Great Britain
by Amazon